PRAISE FOR ANTON CANCRE

Nice things cool people said about this book:

Cancre creates stanzas that feel like dark, lush landscapes and dense thickets hiding secrets and fears; pieces that feel organic like the cold night sky, yet tell stories of the systemic societal and familial breakdowns that happen beneath it.

The nightmares have spilled out of the individual mind and now roam the streets.

These poems remind you that no one is safe, inside or out.

— Donna Lynch *Choking Back the Devil, Witches, Isabel Burning*

Lines and sudden feelings stick out like the proverbial bone in skin.

— ZZ Claybourne, author of *Afropuffs are the Antennae of the Universe*

Nice things cool people said about Anton Cancre:

Anton is a word wizard weaving images of nightmares in such simple, sharp combinations.

— Donna Munro, author of Revelation (book 1 of the Poppet Cycle)

I feel a sentient presence, obstinate and irreverent, as Cancre's poems unfold.

-Marge Simon, multiple Bram Stoker Award winning, grand master poet, SFPA.

THIS STORY DOESN'T END THE WAY WE WANT ALL THE TIME

Lesley,

NOT EVERY LIGHT AT THE END OF THE TUNNEL IS AN ONCOMING TRAIN.

— ANTON

LANURE

THIS STORY DOESN'T END THE WAY WE WANT ALL THE TIME

ANTON CANCRE

This Story Doesn't End The Way We Want All The Time is published by Dragon's Roost Press

Copyright © 2021 by Anton Cancre

Cover Art by Steven Archer

All rights reserved.

No part of this book may be reproduced in any form or by any electronic or mechanical means, including information storage and retrieval systems, without written permission from the author, except for the use of brief quotations in a book review.

Printed in the United States of America

First Printing 2021

Paperback ISBN: 978-1-956824-99-5

Dragon's Roost Press

207 Gardendale

Ferndale, MI 48220

This book is dedicated to every cosplayer, youtuber, game critic, fanfiction writer, homespun game dev, indie filmmaker, and fan that keeps these fog-shrouded streets snaking off into new and exciting realms. I love you all.

CONTENTS

Foreword	xiii
TheGamingMuse	
Untitled	xvii
Intro:	1
SECTION I: LOST IN THE FOG	3
Born in Fire	5
Awoke In Flame	7
Mother, Dearest	9
A Disregard of Genetics	11
To Do No Harm	13
You Never Did Anything	15
Mother Figure	17
SECTION II:	19
Screams, Like Sirens, From the Air	21
Best Friends, Howling for Blood	23
Smiles Like Knives	25
Black Wisps and Giggles	27
Devoured in the Choking Heat	29
Playing Doctor	31
Mumbling in the Dark	33
Larval Form	35
Born to Fly	37
Lurking Amid Drips and Shadows	39
Tools Once Useful Do Not Merely Disappear	41
Cycles Don't Have to Be Natural to be Insistent	43
SECTION III:	45
School	47
Police Station	49
Hospital	51
Town Center	53
Lighthouse	55

Amusement Park	57
Nowhere	59
SECTION IV:	61
The Crash	63
On the Dream of Waking	65
Children, Laughing	67
On The Waking of a Dream	69
Off to See the Wizard	71
Monsters in this Deeper Dark Borne	73
The Secret Shame of Bathroom Stalls	75
Open Time's Door to Beckon Prey	77
A Friend in Need	79
A Friend Indeed	81
Sun in an Old Man's Palm	83
Just a Cat	85
The Moon Held Back by Songless Birds	87
Notice: Hell Is Coming	89
Awakening the Hungry Beast	91
The Good Doctor, Shaken	93
Down the Rabbit Hole	95
The Basement's Basement	97
A Green Lion, Eating the Sun	99
The Truth of the Old Church	101
Some Other World, Like a Bad Dream	103
Devoured by Darkness	105
Help Me, Daddy	107
Not Supposed to Leave This Place	109
One Kind Face	111
The Only Way Over is Under	113
A Fusing of Reality and Nightmare	115
What Mommy Said in the Dark	117
You Must Stop the Demon	119
I Have to Save Her	121
Round and Round We Go	123
I Will Do Anything	125
Let's Go Home Now	127
Path of Angels	129

The Same as Them	131
White Claudia, or the Light Illuminating the Darkness	133
A Room Full of Eyes	135
Where is the Soul?	137
Returned to Her Former Self	139
Angel of Righteous Fury	141
Aglaophotis and Demon	143
The Venom of God	145
A Prophecy Fulfilled	147
The Physics of Self-Harm and Equilibrium	149
Alchemical Metamorphosis	151
With the Sundering, as with Birth, Pain	153
Acknowledgments	155
About the Author	157
About Dragon's Roost Press	159
Also by Anton Cancre	161

FOREWORD

THEGAMINGMUSE

When Anton reached out to me about writing an introduction to his book of poetry centered upon the first *Silent Hill* game, I was delighted. Poetry? For *Silent Hill*? No game could possibly better inspire more haunting, strange, and eclectic works of art than this one.

Reading them, I was not at all disappointed. Each one felt like stepping back onto those fog laden streets – like seeing the cutscenes of the game all over again, from another angle, or point of view. A condensed, intense expression of feeling that was always there in the game that's been brought to new life through the written word.

Imagery from the game is brought to life in such clear-cut language, pulling on images the player has undoubtedly seen, describing them in a way that gives them new depth – the 'screaming air that brings the change' immediately calling the siren and the Otherworld to mind without ever naming either. There is a haunting dreamlike quality to the poems, the way they shift points of view, who is speaking and who is the audience. The use of lines and language from the games in new ways gives double the impact of multiple lines, speaking in a language only *Silent Hill* fans will fully understand.

There's so little to look forward to, as *Silent Hill* fans. Konami's abandoned us and more and more it seems only conspiracy theories seem to entice fans. We need to start looking to our own to create new *Silent Hill* content; to writers like Anton, who has turned the experience of the first *Silent Hill* game into a series of deep, dark breaths interspersed with the silence that comes with the flip of a new page, of short poetic stories to tell yourself in the dark, read by the light of a flashlight.

This Story Doesn't End the Way We Want All the Time – how horribly true. *Silent Hill* the series has ended as a controversy and a cancelled project. *Silent Hill* ends either with the death of the protagonist, or at best, the loss of his first child. Things don't go the way we want, all too often. But at least here, *Silent Hill* fans can find a comforting return to form, to the horror and mystery that first drew them to that dreary town, presented in a new way.

If you've been looking for another way to return to that special place; if you've longed for something new to scratch the ever-present itch for the horrors of the mind; if you miss *Silent Hill*, look no further than this, for a way to return there once again, in a new familiar and unfamiliar way, to feel the presence of those shadows pressing in, to hear the creaks and feel the madness within.

The story may not end the way we want, but you'll certainly enjoy the ride.

-TGM

Foreword

Muse is a writer, researcher, and streamer with a Silent Hill obsession and a love of all things horror. You can find his books on his ko-fi store, and his Silent Hill Symbolism videos, exploring the mythos of the series, on his youtube channel.

Store: *https://ko-fi.com/thegamingmuse*

CW:
Some poems in this book may be considered violent or cruel.

INTRO:

WHAT THE SIREN HERALDS IN THIS DENSE UNLIGHT

The fog, this haze of buried

memory, doesn't destroy anything.

Not in a place like this. No,

the dense, heavy drops of water,

clinging to the dust of old,

microscopic hurts just obscure

the truth, refract the light back

and away into meaningless white

noise. But the balance of stasis

is a precarious one, a tiptoe

pirouette on the head of a pin

with only a minute shift in

temperature to bring it all crashing

ANTON CANCRE

down in icy torrents and bring

the stark, void-black terror

of what was screaming into view.

SECTION I:

THOSE LOST IN THE FOG

BORN IN FIRE

Swaddled and resting

on the side of the road

when he found her.

The sole, small

remainder of love,

of hope for something

more than pain, than anger.

A seed of a dream

to be carried on the wind

and find root in cleaner soil

than the crimson soaked

sacrificial mud of the Hill.

AWOKE IN FLAME

Swaddled and screaming

in the dark of the cell

where they left her.

A swelling, putrescent

goiter of agony,

of hatred for everything

less than hope, than adoration.

A kernel of nightmare

to soak into the soil

and poison the prayers

stained crimson in the

sacrificial mud of the Hill

MOTHER, DEAREST

The one face seen every morning, spilling

name after name of ancients rites and rituals

for the rising of a once discarded but not forgotten

god. The focus of our daily existence, not found

in mundane degrees of happiness bouncing

the joyful lilt of laughter but instead pulling

lips downward into dour serious intent bent

and centered on the cultivating and use of a

hearts deepest held strength. Not one look

of love but filled instead with the deep emerald of

little demons screaming for the bitter use of

children this face was meant to protect against.

A DISREGARD OF GENETICS

There are times when that acid
which claims to hold the keys of lineage
and tribal ties only eats away
at the rungs of its own twisted ladder,
when, conversely, distant degrees
of biological incongruence intertwine
knots of inescapable affection so that,
on the collapse of reason and
the realization of the lies or the past,
the only possible thing that may remain
is a man's love for his daughter.

TO DO NO HARM

There's a promise

in the uniform, a promise

in the sign on the door, a promise

in the paper framed and hung on the office wall.

An implication that health

and well being come before

all else, especially

greed. But we

all know better

than that, now.

Don't we?

YOU NEVER DID ANYTHING

The healer, cloaked

in crimson and downcast

eyes, bearing sly simian

weight upon her shoulders

and a crown of pale-petaled

flowers over her brow.

You never asked

for this, but those

kind lips, pursed

in perpetual sympathy,

never once found

the strength to say no.

MOTHER FIGURE

Dressed to the hilt

in black and blue,

the trappings of

authority all over again,

the child of fire sees

where this is going

even as the newborn

light reaches out for her.

Mother has never been

a kind word and she sees

the mindless, senseless

violence shambling her way:

the swift backhand crack

for getting too close

and the scalding

lead kisses blown from afar.

No gentle caresses

or kind words rest here

as the circle spins back around.

SECTION II:

THE VICIOUS GHOSTS THAT STILL PATROL THESE DEPTHS

SCREAMS, LIKE SIRENS, FROM THE AIR

They come first in flutters,

in light, airy rustles, the soft

scrape of flitting pages

but any joy in this nostalgia

dies quickly with the screams

that follow, diving out of the fog

of the past with claws

and teeth bent on rending.

An early reminder

that even those things

that once kept us safe

want nothing but blood

when we return to them.

BEST FRIENDS, HOWLING FOR BLOOD

They are supposed to love

everyone, but what

does that mean anyways?

When the one word

that was supposed to mean

love twists itself inward

and out before your eyes, there

should not be room

for shock and forms inverted

to raw scabs and bared teeth.

Even the best of friends

have no choice but to turn vicious

in times like these.

SMILES LIKE KNIVES

We're told so often of their innocence
that we tend to forget what they are,
what they do. We let slide into blank
recesses the shouts and the curses
and the casual cruelty. There are times,
still, though, when gleaming white
smiles float to the surface, sharpened
teeth cutting through everything
and setting these old scars to itching.

BLACK WISPS AND GIGGLES

They almost seem cute.

Stumbling and squeaking

in their harmless way.

Anyone would be forgiven

for falling for the lie. But,

there's something

to the faint outline of smokey,

chubby darkness, a tangible

void against the already

oppressive emptiness

that stirs a memory I don't

want to deal with right now.

DEVOURED IN THE CHOKING HEAT

Closed-faced and jutting,

the beast lurks

in flames of the deeper

emptiness. A story

from the long lost past

that refuses to go away.

Hooded. Concealed. It

slams over and over

into flesh that yields

too easily, only showing

its softness when

lunging in for the kill.

PLAYING DOCTOR

I suppose they all remind me

of him, now. Hunched and mumbling

threats disguised as mercy.

Wielding ragged and rusty tools

of rage that don't even pretend

to the healing arts.

Those bulbous mounds pulsating

on their backs were never needed

for me to read their malicious intent.

MUMBLING IN THE DARK

So many stories

warned us of them,

speaking of their

greater evil waiting

for those who dared

stray from the path.

So many children

stolen for food

or worse when they

refused to listen

to guiding words

when offered. Those

stories never warned

ANTON CANCRE

that home, too, can

sometimes be their warren.

LARVAL FORM

Ghost pallid, undulating

in segments of plump,

pulsating flesh, it worries

the soil beneath. Gorging

on concrete and, likely,

more than its fair share

of bones, it grows

fat and anxious. Spewing

bile, it will find its own

way to freedom along

the path I no longer feel

I am choosing. Such passages,

painful as they may be,

are sometimes necessary.

BORN TO FLY

Freed from the depths now,
and metamorphosed, this living
flutter of pallid, powdered wings
and carapace has finally become
what it was always meant to be.
And still, the same acidic bile
spills from its lips, rotting
whatever it touches. And still,
it falls into the same trap
of attack with no value
to be found in victory. And still,
there is no escape, even if
the cage is larger. The only

ANTON CANCRE

new trick it has learned comes

at the barbed end of a tail

spiked with poison, impaled.

LURKING AMID DRIPS AND SHADOWS

Youth, in it's naive

cruelty, can be capable

of the worst crimes.

Green carapaced bodies

impaled, squirming and squealing,

pleading in their own alien tongues

for some form of mercy. But,

sometimes, we find the world

inverted and the opportunity

arises for the skewering

to be on the other hand.

There is no reasonable

expectation of mercy, then.

TOOLS ONCE USEFUL DO NOT MERELY DISAPPEAR

In the dark, beneath

the basement, I learned

her strength. In

the flames, while flesh

melted off of me

in waves of slick wax,

she taught me how

to redirect the fire

and burn those around me.

Her wings wrapped,

cool and comforting around

me while we both

dreamt of destruction and I

ANTON CANCRE

found the only

measure of safety I could trust.

It doesn't come

as much of a surprise that I

can hear her calling again.

CYCLES DON'T HAVE TO BE NATURAL TO BE INSISTENT

When you take the mantle

of the first voice heard, it

is worth knowing what words

fell from that mouth. It

is worth knowing that

repetition is expected

and when her viciousness

is not made immediately

apparent, measures will

be taken to bring it

to the surface. In the end,

we'll see that I was right

even if your hand is forced.

SECTION III:

SAFE SPACES GONE SOUR

SCHOOL

The halls bear less

light than they should,

twisted into this convoluted

knot of dead ends

and locked doors,

the way through barred

in dense rhyme and metaphor.

Squealing amid it all,

the shadows of dead

dreams trip over

their own feet, clambering

to dig their teeth into mine

and the bright barbs

of giggling children

ANTON CANCRE

whet themselves in the hope

of tasting weakness.

The lessons learned

here are earned in

the blood that paints the walls.

POLICE STATION

It's the place

you're supposed to go

to when there's trouble.

The home of uniformed friends.

"Don't worry, dear,"

the posters at school used to say,

"you can tell us anything

and we'll keep you safe."

Except for when they don't

and you find yourself back

at the same shameful door

and that plastic barbie smile

is stretched across her face

ANTON CANCRE

full of nods and apologies

and sincere thanks

for your return and you

finally know for sure that it

will only get worse from here.

HOSPITAL

Mama said they all
made a promise here.
That they all swore to it
when they walked
through the doors, but here
we are in the deep dark
halls where hunch-backed
doctors lurk with their stainless
steel cutting implements,
begging to strip away
the healthy flesh until nothing
but rot remains and I
can almost hear the mold

ANTON CANCRE

growing between cracks

in the broken tiling whisper

the lie in refrain: to do no harm.

TOWN CENTER

She's screaming through static'd
screens where ads once
gleefully shilled nonsense, locked
in a two dimensional cry for help.
It's the binding that does it, not
in the receipt paper of spent joy
or in the bright ribbon to be passed
along, but in stinking, sodden cloth.
All the stores have gone now,
but something pale and hungry
burrows in the foundations.

LIGHTHOUSE

This was a beacon
once, for when the fog
became too thick and
those lost on the lake
feared to never find
their way home. But
the light here has since
sputtered out, as light
everywhere eventually
does, leaving nothing
but an empty spiral
of darkness. A firefly
cry for help that falls
as flat as the stilled waves.

AMUSEMENT PARK

This used to be our playground,
where we ran and screamed
and puked in abject joy. Only
now, the running is not *to* anything,
but *from* everything. Shadowed
forms of lost children hound
the corners, whose squeaks
and squeals rival the rusted
scrape of metal from the rides
and whose own steel is nearly
as finely honed. Worse, still,
is what threatens to erupt
from a barely restrained gullet.

NOWHERE

It's always been this way
inside, these unlit corridors
doubling back onto themselves,
the utter disregard for linearity
of time and space. All of it
existing as one, at once, stacked
and looped, self-devouring
and filled with beasts bent
on tearing and flaying and sinking
whatever bits of edged anger
they possess into you.
The way out is not through,
because there is no way out.

SECTION IV:
IN THE PLACE OF SILENT SPIRITS

THE CRASH

She came

out of nowhere,

as long lost things

tend to do.

Too sudden,

too ephemeral

to be, but solid,

returning borrowed

light to my eyes.

There wasn't time

to think, barely enough

to react before the world

upended, twisting and

spinning and tumbling

ANTON CANCRE

until the canceling out

of conflicting inertias.

The screech of tearing

metal in a spray of broken

shards refracting the lost

light in a thousand directions

before silence and the darkness

of invading night.

ON THE DREAM OF WAKING

An eventual slide into consciousness
does not always come with illumination.
Case in point: this meandering
through strange, unlit streets
to chase down the shadow of a girl
that might have been, these footsteps
that echo in the fog. Could it be her?
Could it be me? As the deeper dark
descends and the flame in my hand
melts the snow to a warm drizzle,
as the bodies lining the streets drip
their pain into nothingness as barbed
wired crucifixions point the way.

ANTON CANCRE

The blood splashed ground bodes
no good will, that much is clear.

CHILDREN, LAUGHING

Laughter is not

particularly welcome

in times like these.

Less so the appearance

of children baring

sharp blades like grins

and backing me up

against the rusted

lattice of old chain link.

Neither is the realization

that there is nowhere

left to run.

ON THE WAKING OF A DREAM

It's too quick, too

sharp, like the intrusion

of steel into flesh, this

abrupt drop into

existence amid the

distant buzz of neon

and the flutter of

fleshy wings against

the window. The

liminality of dreaming

should not be honed

to such a harmful point.

OFF TO SEE THE WIZARD

It's always easy to step

your first feet onto the path,

when the night has yet

to deepen and the air

lies unrent by hate-filled

screeches and desperate howls.

The golden, symmetrical

simplicity of bricks in even

lines has yet to twist,

to diverge, to hide its truth

in obtuse unreason.

There has been no struggle

against the clear call to violence

with a bare, open hand.

ANTON CANCRE

The time of such trials may
be inevitable, but they loom
so small on the horizon that
it is easy to diminish them
further while whistling
an uneasy tune.

MONSTERS IN THIS DEEPER DARK BORNE

Something more

is held here, subsumed

by the high wails

of sirens heralding

a descent to a deeper dark.

Something that

slavers and growls

in the dim distance.

Something of teeth

and claws and

raw, seeping red flesh.

Something that hungers

to reduce us all to nothing.

THE SECRET SHAME OF BATHROOM STALLS

Cheap aluminum dividers,

scored with the harsh wit

and biting wisdom of years

long past, and cracked tile

only serve to echo my sobs

back at me, twisting them

to cruel mockery. There's no

comfort to be found here,

steeped in stale urine and

shit, but I can think of no place

more fitting to contemplate

a lack of place in the world.

OPEN TIME'S DOOR TO BECKON PREY

Sometimes, it doesn't
heal, this endless loop
of sun and moon
reigniting flames not quite
extinguished and tearing
open forgotten wounds.
Sometimes, it just
brings you back to the place
you worked so hard
to escape, an inward
spiralling trap gilded with pretty
promises of hope that
slick the coils, removing

ANTON CANCRE

all option of retreat while through

seems less a matter

of getting out than a way in.

A FRIEND IN NEED

She's here

somewhere.

I'm here

somewhere.

Trapped behind

rusted grating and

the high, endless scream

of sirens in the distance

where the dark bares

sharpened teeth but it's

hard to find the breath

to call for help when

choking on the dust

of someone else's dreams.

A FRIEND INDEED

Sometimes

there is a realization

waiting

in the simplicity of

cliches,

hidden in the basic

bland

nonsense of boring

ass,

mass produced motivational

posters

papering the walls.

Sometimes,

a request is left unvoiced, a

ANTON CANCRE

desire

for aid choked back

behind

desperation and terror and a

blind

belief that the now is

all

that can possibly exist.

Sometimes,

the other hand has to be

extended

first and, even then, we

may

not know how to accept it.

SUN IN AN OLD MAN'S PALM

The bright light of the future,

a torch and the path and

the one way forward held tight

in the grip of a withered palm,

cold and unyielding as stone.

A hold broken only by

judicious application of

the water of a sage's wisdom.

With a bubble and a crack

and a puff of acrid smoke,

the first brief glimpse of the sun's

rays are free to shine through.

JUST A CAT

Repetitive yowls

and thumps

and it just

wants to be

set free.

A simple enough

request granted

easily.

But what

is one to do

when it rounds

the corner and

the squeal

ANTON CANCRE

squelches with wet

finality, echoing

the truth of freedom?

THE MOON HELD BACK BY SONGLESS BIRDS

The Moon Held Back by Songless Birds

It's absurd to think

of calling down the moon

with discordant cries

of voiceless birds,

and following the path of blood

in clunky arrhythmic

hops set to unrhymed poetry

but the sky refuses to come,

even when the night falls.

NOTICE: HELL IS COMING

Well over

to the wrong side

of the rainbow, hemmed

in by rusted razorwire

fencing and hounded

by the well-honed blades

of pale children.

I feel like

the posted sign,

even in this place of warded

non-healing, falls far too

late to do anyone any good.

AWAKENING THE HUNGRY BEAST

Back to the burning. It
always seems to come
back to that. In this place
where the beast and
I dance around the pillar
of flame, each of us
spinning gently, thrusting,
probing for a spot
of weakness, hoping
that, this time, he
will be the one
to open wide, exposing
soft innards to be torn free.

THE GOOD DOCTOR, SHAKEN

I'll admit a certain joy
in seeing you there,
that smug stoicism
knocked from your face
for even the smallest moment,
to see that slight twitch
and shudder as you finally
have to face a few
of the monsters,
these aberrations you finally
acknowledge should have
never existed, that you
worked so hard to create.

DOWN THE RABBIT HOLE

It's where we jump
down the rabbit hole,
where simple bedside tales
take over and reshape
the world, diving beneath
the dirt to escape
the flames, the pain.
A place where mom
becomes the screaming
queen of blood and severed
heads and that damn
doctor with his mad grin
gets to don his fancy hats

ANTON CANCRE

while spouting his nonsense

and I...

well I get to play the kitty

with the enigmatic smile,

leading the little girl on to victory.

THE BASEMENT'S BASEMENT

We keep

these things secreted away,

deep down,

behind locked doors covered with

overlooked

cabinets, hoping that they won't

get out

but bits seep through the grate,

overgrown

with knotted weeds as it may be,

reaching out

to pollute the surface.

A GREEN LION, EATING THE SUN

Everything stays polished

here, gleaming clean

despite the apparent disorder.

A sanctuary of relics

from our forgotten past

when the reed and the snake

both shown bright

in the sun before both

night and we, with it, fall.

Wax and work, the grease

of strained elbows, are needed

in abundance to maintain

the illusion that no deeper fears

lay hidden in the cracks.

THE TRUTH OF THE OLD CHURCH

Behind the cracks, hidden

in the far back by a curio

built to hold curios, we

used to crawl to the space

of true belief and yes, we

ignored what we knew and we

both knew no god walked

here amid bare pipes and

stained cement but still

mother burned the darkness

back with her candles

and begged for something

better on her knees.

SOME OTHER WORLD, LIKE A BAD DREAM

The screaming air that
brings the change, the shift
and descent into clarity
and emptiness. It's like
another world opening up,
a bad dream, a negation
of reality sirens call
from nothing and bared
metal drips with rust
and blood and foul beasts
turned inside out, glistening,
howling to reduce me
to my component parts.

. . .

ANTON CANCRE

Please,

tell me you've seen it,

too.

DEVOURED BY DARKNESS

This place of silence, slipping

noisily into her maw, jagged,

rust-toothed and gaping

to swallow it all down to some

lower deep, always waiting.

Those points when she

forces it all further down to

the places where cruelty hides.

Places too near a center that

no longer holds but slips

its tendrils into and through

the barest cracks in the foundation,

pressing them open further.

HELP ME, DADDY

Something isn't right in me.
Hasn't been for longer
than I care to admit. It twitches
and writhes inside, rising
like worms or flames
that threaten to devour me.
I don't know who I am anymore.
I feel a call from some place
long buried, a past best forgotten
rising up. Something new
is surfacing, coming in
to blurry definition through the murk
and I'm scared that I won't be me
when all is said and done.

NOT SUPPOSED TO LEAVE THIS PLACE

Poor Lisa knows. I can
see it in her eyes. Regardless
of the denials and the protestations
of the opposite, she has no doubt
that her hope is futile. She's
bathed too much in blood, lived
too long in the dark, to honestly
believe that any happy ending
could be in the cards for her.
She's too tied, even in regret,
to the slippery goons down
the hall and to the dull
blades they carry. There

ANTON CANCRE

will be no leaving this place,

dearest Lisa knows.

ONE KIND FACE

In the days after the fire
worked so hard to burn away
everything that I was,
in the dark of the basement's
basement, buried away
from prying eyes and the light
of hope, Lisa was there.
With a smile stretched
across her face and a gentle
word, she was always there.
She almost screamed
when he had to change
the bandages, to wash away

ANTON CANCRE

the ooze and rot before it

set in too deep, but she

still spoke only of calm joy.

I kept a special spot

in my private hell for her.

THE ONLY WAY OVER IS UNDER

The shortest distance
between two points
is, at times like these,
often sundered and
where the cracks cannot
be leapt, another path
must be sought.
Then, when the surface
is too fraught with peril,
we sometimes have to
grab a shovel or just
find a convenient tunnel
to see what depths may
bypass our blockades.

A FUSING OF REALITY AND NIGHTMARE

There comes a point

in our tales, dear friends,

where the artifice must

be stripped away.

A moment where the paltry,

flashy window dressing must

succumb to the rot of reality

and the cold, rusted bones

of the world are laid bare.

Where the lies of hope

fade into the uncaring

void and no light can be

found to guide us. Only

ANTON CANCRE

then can we see ourselves

as we truly are.

WHAT MOMMY SAID IN THE DARK

Mommy, mommy has some things to say
about what grows inside.
Mommy, mommy doesn't approve.

Mommy, mommy's seen the blood
red symbology scrawled.
Mommy, mommy knows better.

Mommy, mommy understands
the truth
beneath the surface lies.
Mommy, mommy whispers their names.

. . .

ANTON CANCRE

Mommy, mommy says it's evil that makes me this way.

mommy, mommy said this must be done.

YOU MUST STOP THE DEMON

It's a simple enough mandate
from a simple enough source,
all cliche enough to fit
into a nice, neat little box.
All wrapped up so cleanly.
Just a frail old woman asking
the obvious from her tough,
strapping hero. We all know
where this leads, where it
has to go. So much so,
in fact, that I can't help asking
myself what stake she has
in the fight and how much I
really should be listening to her.

I HAVE TO SAVE HER

There has to come a point
where you acknowledge
that you've come to a point
where turning back, walking
away is no longer an option.
The place where the blood
spent has become too precious
and the desperate screams
have filled too many rooms.
Even lost in this empty chaos
of violence and noise she built,
there is the need to believe
that salvation is an option.

ROUND AND ROUND WE GO

The fancy plastic horses
know the deal: the faster
we go, the clearer it becomes.
They've seen her here before,
bruised and giant barbie smiling
her way through the ride.
Whispering in their shellacked ears
to kick it up, please, just a little
bit more. Then they'll all break
loose. Then she'll finally be free
of this. But she's finally come
to understand what they tried to
convey in their twisted, carved

ANTON CANCRE

rictus, that every circle will

eventually close back in on itself.

I WILL DO ANYTHING

It's easy enough

to say. Five syllables

that practically throw

themselves from willing

enough lips. From

the comfort of sane

symplicity, though, they

boil down to meaningless

grunts, signifying nothing.

It's when the world finds

itself wrapped in blood

and hatred, pulled into nothing

by the rage of misdirected

terror that the truth shines.

How much are your words worth?

LET'S GO HOME NOW

This is the truth,
here, in splinter-sharp steel
and the ceaseless wailing
of a starless sky, in a horizon
festooned with barbed-wired
bound corpses leaking their last
into rotting grates of eternity.
The truth lies in pain, received
and given back in kind. Any
imagined respite in shining light
and love, in comfort and care,
was only a cruel dream to be
broken on the crack of an eye.

ANTON CANCRE

It's time to return to

the only home I've ever known.

PATH OF ANGELS

These dense, winding
paths have purpose,
please do not doubt this.
There is The Way
and only The Way,
to end in judgement
and peace. The fluttering
of invisible wings
told me as much.
A certain beauty can
be found in the warped
carnality of it all, if
you can only bend
your ear to the lessons

imparted from the razor
edges lining the walls.
Yes, the indecision can
turn even the most stalwart
to stone, should you let
confusion and apathy sink
in, but even that bare
stone can bear fruit
under the right tutelage.

THE SAME AS THEM

It's easy to say
you are better, that
reason is yours alone
while the rest flail
in bloody ignorance.
Beasts bound by blind
instinct to rend and tear,
wounding for only
some inscrutable instinct.
That your only aim
was to help. But, enough
time down in the dark,
Downing the bile
that pours from faucets

ANTON CANCRE

while steel squeals down

the hall, edges sharpening

in anticipation of use,

forces a brand of honesty

not found in the light,

an understanding that,

regardless of intent,

the results were the same.

WHITE CLAUDIA, OR THE LIGHT ILLUMINATING THE DARKNESS

Sometimes, clarity is needed.

I think we can all agree on that.

Something to wash away

the chaff and noise closing

in from every angle.

Sometimes, a bite or two

of Alice's cake is needed

to place it all in perspective,

to give us all the distance we

need or allow a closer glance.

Those who hid their selfish

bloodlust and greed behind

bleached smocks do not necessarily

ANTON CANCRE

negate apothecary wisdom

of external chemicals in helping us

identify our dearest held demons.

A ROOM FULL OF EYES

Call it paranoid if you will. You
wouldn't be the first. Still, I
feel them resting on me
constantly, measuring my sins
by spoonfuls just as I feel
the undulating reverberations
of compressed air hissing
of torn flesh and the escape
of inevitability. There is a desire
to separate souls from skin
scrawled into the walls
and a small, quiet voice
begging for assistance and exit.

WHERE IS THE SOUL?

Such ephemera cannot remain whole
through some ordeals. Like smoke,
they scatter, sifting like oil and stones
in water. Some bits float to the surface,
shining bright in the gentle light
of the sun and returning nearly as much
as they receive. Others sink down deep
where the light itself fears to dwell,
learning to soak up nothing but absence
while giving the same back unto the world.
On occasion, tumult can bring
these hidden bits to the surface, muddying
the whole ordeal while we prefer to pretend
that the calm surface is all there is to see.

RETURNED TO HER FORMER SELF

There is no forgetting. Moving
on or past is only an illusion.
Regardless of time passed,
of the weight of years holding
dawn at bay, that which was
buried will always eventually
find its way back to the surface.
With it, old grudges, old hates,
old fears will find themselves
at the helm raining blood and terror
over everything. Your dancing
girl will find her way home again.

ANGEL OF RIGHTEOUS FURY

Even in this dim

void, my fury glows

bright as the white

hot light of God's

own truth, blinding,

burning the air

with crackling thunder.

My only hope, my only

friend in suffering. My

salvation, twisting

the flames to my own will.

AGLAOPHOTIS AND DEMON

A thick red

tincture, so like

blood amid

the shards of broken

glass, a philosopher's

poultice, a ward,

to burn away

consuming flames

and quelch the blinding

light of heavenly grace

to reveal the fallen form.

THE VENOM OF GOD

It's a poison,

a death by degrees

that resides within

a cannibalistic flame

feeding reflexively

while cajoling with

the syrupy-sweet

voice of the sky.

There is no hope

of shelter beneath

these wings, nor truth

to the promises

of ascension only

ANTON CANCRE

the desire to leave

all as dust, scattered

to nihil and void.

A PROPHECY FULFILLED

Are you proud yet, dear,

now that I've fulfilled

your self-imposed prophecy,

borne the fruit you so

selfishly desired? Have I

finally become what

you bred me to be? Earned

the blood shed in payment?

Do you approve, finally,

as your own flesh withers

and blisters under hands

you never deigned to caress?

THE PHYSICS OF SELF-HARM AND EQUILIBRIUM

It's a sad truth that,

sometimes,

the only answer to violence

is more of the same.

Equal opposing forces and all of that.

Interior struggles differ

no more, in that regard, than exterior ones.

Our demons, after all,

deal in blood and sacrifice.

Pleas of love and forgiveness

neither appease nor absolve them.

And so we find ourselves engulfed

in thunder and lightning,

ANTON CANCRE

in exchanges of energy

until one or both

are exhausted in the other.

ALCHEMICAL METAMORPHOSIS

There are points where

that which shines brightest

does not, in truth, light our way.

Lights at the end of the tunnel

revealing themselves to be

the headlamps of oncoming trains

or our angel, our salvation,

showing itself shorn of wings

with the right tincture. Correct

Chemicals stripping away

the false glow to reveal fangs

and claws and the beast within

whispering the sundering of all.

WITH THE SUNDERING, AS WITH BIRTH, PAIN

With enough force, the light
can be brought forth. The illusions
that bound the past can be torn
down in righteous flame. But void
cannot be replaced with void, nor
nihil with nihil, lest the same damn
circle spin continuous with no
forward movement. If we want
our devils replaced with something
more, we have to strive to build it
ourselves. Our new future born
not against the past, but
incorporating it into some new child.

ACKNOWLEDGMENTS

Thanks:

This book owes a huge debt to CVXFreak (who wrote the first in-depth analysis of Silent Hill I ever read), TheGamingMuse, and Ragnarrox for getting me to look at this fever dream from different angles. Of course, I wouldn't have had anything to obsess over, if not for the art, insight, skill, and drive of the original Team Silent: Keiichiro Toyama, Masahiro Ito, Takayoshi Sato, Masashi Tsuboyama, Hiroyuki Owaku, Gozo Kitao, and Akihiro Imamura.

ABOUT THE AUTHOR

Anton Cancre's mother wasn't really pregnant with him when she went to see The Exorcist, but he tells people that anyways because it sounds cool. He's had poetry published in *Space and Time* magazine, the *Horror Zine* and *Nothing's Sacred*. He's also a luddite who still has a blogspot website (antoncancre.blogspot.com) and runs the Spec Griot Garage podcast (specgriotgarage.podbean.com) where he gets to gush over other people's poems with cool folks.

ABOUT DRAGON'S ROOST PRESS

Dragon's Roost Press is the fever dream brainchild of dark speculative fiction author Michael Cieslak. Since 2014, their goal has been to find the best speculative fiction authors and share their work with the public. For more information about Dragon's Roost Press and their publications, please visit:

Dragon's Roost Press

For more great horror, please check out our new website:

http://www.thedragonsroost.biz

ALSO BY ANTON CANCRE

Meaningless Cycles in a Vicious Glass Prison: Songs of Death and Love

We live. We die. About a week later, we get back up and start tearing the flesh off of whoever is most convenient to fill the emptiness in our bacteria-bloated corpses that is most definitely not a metaphor of our desperate search for connection in this hopeless slog of repetitive day to day existence. Sometimes, there's sex and/or blood.

Made in the USA
Columbia, SC
22 August 2022